ADVENTURES OF AKUA AND HER FRIENDS

Akua Adoma Baffoe-Bonnie

Copyright © 2021 Akua Adoma Baffoe-Bonnie.

All rights reserved. No part of this book may be used or reproduced by any means, graphic, electronic, or mechanical, including photocopying, recording, taping or by any information storage retrieval system without the written permission of the author except in the case of brief quotations embodied in critical articles and reviews.

This is a work of fiction. All of the characters, names, incidents, organizations, and dialogue in this novel are either the products of the author's imagination or are used fictitiously.

LifeRich Publishing is a registered trademark of The Reader's Digest Association, Inc.

LifeRich Publishing books may be ordered through booksellers or by contacting:

LifeRich Publishing
1663 Liberty Drive
Bloomington, IN 47403
www.liferichpublishing.com
844-686-9607

Because of the dynamic nature of the Internet, any web addresses or links contained in this book may have changed since publication and may no longer be valid. The views expressed in this work are solely those of the author and do not necessarily reflect the views of the publisher, and the publisher hereby disclaims any responsibility for them.

Any people depicted in stock imagery provided by Getty Images are models, and such images are being used for illustrative purposes only.
Certain stock imagery © Getty Images.

ISBN: 978-1-4897-3455-6 (sc)
ISBN: 978-1-4897-3456-3 (e)

Print information available on the last page.

LifeRich Publishing rev. date: 03/26/2021

CONTENTS

Dedication v

Acknowledgements vii

Prologue ix

Little Akua and her Stranger Friend 1

Akua and the Coconut Tress 7

Akua, Soso and Copycat Parrot go to the Market 15

DEDICATION

This book is dedicated to my Parents, Family and Friends

ACKNOWLEDGEMENTS

Thank you to my parents who gave me the best start in life and have always been there for me, to family and friends who encouraged and gave me a belief in myself.

Mrs Sue Phillips – thank you for your encouragement, fearless advice to me, creative direction, a pillar on which I constantly lean and encouragement to accomplish my goal.

Mrs Vivienne Roberts – thank you for your steadfast support, encouragement and reminding me always of a "can do" attitude.

PROLOGUE

Akua lives on a plantation in Ghana and makes a new friend who is very kind to her and becomes part of the family. Her new friend gives her a gift she cherishes and comes to love.

Little Akua and her Stranger Friend

Written by Akua Adoma

Akua lives with her Mum, Dad and sister in the middle of a rubber plantation in Ghana.

Akua can see trees for miles. She can see men called tappers who tap the trees for its sap. Sap is a white liquid hidden behind the bark of the rubber tree. The tappers make a hole in the bark and sap runs out into a bowl. The tapper collects all the sap together and takes it to a large factory in a huge truck. Her father uses the sap to make tyres and sends them all over the world.

Every morning at six o'clock on the dot, Akua is woken by a lovely tune sung by a happy tapper as he goes by enjoying his job. She is so sure it is the same person because the tune and the voice are the same.

He sings "Oh what a beautiful morning, oh what a beautiful day" till Akua can hear only the echoes and then nothing at all. As the tapper sings, Akua hears the clinggg and the clunkkkkk the tapper's bucket and penknife make. These must be the tools the tapper uses to do his job, Akua thinks to herself. She suddenly shouts, "Good morning!" when she can hardly see or hear him and waits to hear the echo and he then replies the same way! It's such fun!

Mama hears all this going on and thinks it might be nice if they made a cup of tea for her little Akua's friend. She leaves a tray beautifully set up every morning for Kojo the tapper. Kojo helps himself and off he goes again with a clinggg and a clunkkkkk and his beautiful song as usual. Mind you Kojo well deserves that cup of tea as he is up at four each morning tapping the rubber trees for their sap when everyone else is still in bed snoring. He is grateful to Akua's mother for such a kind thought.

This morning though everything is to change. Akua is woken up by a very strange noise that sounds very different today! Akua and her family are going to have a lovely surprise. It is so beautiful this morning the sun is blazing, the birds humming and singing and chickens in the chicken pens at the back of Akua's bedroom clucking in glory as they have just had their breakfast.

Akua suddenly realized it is the teapot and saucers and cups making a noise. She wondered. Could it be Mama having a cup of tea all by herself at this time of the morning? Akua sneaked out of her bedroom on tiptoe to the front door leading to the veranda. "Ah!", she sighed with surprise.

It is a monkey with a white bib, she thought, and he is helping himself to a cup of tea! She could not believe her eyes! Akua ran to tell her mother.

"Mama, Mama you will never believe this! Akua shouted.

"I just saw a monkey drinking a cup of tea on the veranda, and he is wearing a white bib!" she shouts nearly exploding.

"Oh Akua, not one of your funny, daft ideas again!" Mama replied.

"No, Mama it's true!" said Akua in a serious tone.

Mother believes her when she sees the look on Akua's face.
Just then Kojo the tapper knocks on the front door.
"Akua what have you done to the tea tray?" Kojo teased

"I haven't done anything to your tea tray Mr Kojo", shrieked Akua frustrated that no one believed her.

"Oh, yes you have", retorted Kojo pretending he knew nothing about this.

Akua is getting all huffed up now and tries in desperation to get the whole story out. She hardly finishes her sentence and Kojo says in a soft voice, "I believe you, Akua this is our new friend Soso with a lovely white patch down the front of his neck and chest. It does look like a bib doesn't it?" Kojo asked teasingly. "It is a gift from me to you and your family for the kindness you have shown me. You don't know how much I loved your early morning cup of tea" Kojo explained.

Just then Akua's new friend comes striding majestically onto the veranda feeling quite at home and Kojo knows almost immediately he has done the right thing. He knows Soso and Akua will get on like a house on fire and how happy that makes him!

It is tea for three every morning now and what a lovely threesome they make. Soso the monkey plays a new trick every day. He hides Akua's school clothes in the morning and tries to make her late for school but Akua loves him even more.

Soso feels so proud and lucky to have such a lovely caring friend as Akua. Akua's mother turns to Akua and says to her "You know Akua, you made your friend Kojo very happy the day you accepted his present to you. The three had a plan to go to the market together one day.

AKUA AND THE COCONUT TRESS

Written by Akua Adoma

At the back of Akua's bedroom are six very tall and huge coconut trees. The coconut trees are even higher than Akua's house. Under the coconut trees are three chicken coups where Akua's father keeps his chickens for the eggs they lay.

There are always chickens running around chasing and pecking each other, fighting, and tumbling around making such chuckling noises. In the morning Akua often shouts at the chickens when nearly all of them crow and chuckle senselessly at dawn. This is usually as early as four in the morning. "They can't even wait till the sun comes out!" Akua mumbles to herself.

Akua's father, Dada feeds the chickens in the afternoons. This is Akua's favourite part of the day and she skips behind her father in excitement carrying her basket given to her by her mother. Akua's mother, Mama wove it especially for Akua from the leaves of the coconut tree. Akua loves to collect the eggs the chickens have laid for market that day and her father always reminds her to keep some for breakfast.

Akua runs out of patience one morning and she shouts out waking everyone howling and thinking, "I'll pay these chickens back!" "Awoooo, Awoooo, Awooooo!" she yells. Suddenly Akua thinks she hears someone saying the same thing back to her. "Or is she dreaming?" Akua thinks to herself. She yells again, "Awooo, Awooo, AwoooooOOOOOOOO!" Did Akua hear someone yell back again saying "Awooo, Awoooo, Awooooo?" she wondered.

Akua is rather surprised and wonders who that can be. Akua's friend Soso the monkey, is the only one who knows who is copying Akua. He lives up in the coconut trees jumping from one branch to another frightening Akua who is thinking Soso is really taking a chance! Soso often enjoyed doing some very risky jumps and Akua feels her stomach turn over with fright! "If he ever falls it will be terrible", Akua thinks to herself.

Soso has a friend who lives high up in the coconut trees and keeps him company. Parrot is a cheeky fellow. He is such a copycat! He hides up there amongst the branches pretending he is not there and copying everything everyone says. For a time, no one guesses it is Parrot doing his. If anyone hears what sounds like an echo, they think it is just another echo as Akua's house is surrounded by fields, hills and rubber trees and all sorts of noises.

Soso tries several times to try and tell Akua that it is his friend the parrot that is making the same noises every time she speaks. Well you have never seen anything so funny!

Soso starts throwing his hands up in the air, jumping up and down and making the weirdest noises as he tries to tell his friend about the parrot. All Akua can do is laugh till she weeps! "How funny Soso looks" Akua thinks to herself. Mind you by the end of all Soso's cooing, dancing and jumping around, Akua never quite understands what Soso has been trying to tell her. Akua then says to Soso, "I think you better stop all this jumping around before Mama comes and gives us a good telling off."

Mama and Dada are in the kitchen and can hear all that is going on outside. Mama suddenly comes rushing out and asks Akua, "Have you done your chores for the day, Akua?" "No, Mama" replies Akua.

Akua sneaks under the kitchen window and sits in her special spot under the coconut trees. The sun shines right through the branches with such a beautiful glow down on her. Soso sits by Akua for hours when he is not jumping from one branch to another like a crazy monkey, whilst Akua makes brooms from the branches of the coconut trees.

Akua's sister, Ama is an expert at jumping up these elegant trees. Ama climbs up the coconut trees and cuts a few branches ready for broom making. Akua and Ama tear leaves from the veins and gather these to make special brooms for sweeping the compound of her house. This afternoon within a few minutes Akua and Ama had made two brooms, then three, four, five and six! I wonder if all that laughing that got them through their work!

Akua and Ama ran in to the house to show Mama and Dada how fast they had worked today. Mama is so proud of her girls, "At this rate Akua and Ama, we could be running a business soon, well done!" Mama exclaims. The family tuck into their food and no sooner is lunch finished Akua and Ama ran right back to their special spot!

AKUA AND THE COCONUT TRESS

Ama leaves her special spot to feed the chickens. Soso is high amongst the coconut tree branches still making the most unbearable noises Akua has ever heard. "What on earth are you doing up there Soso. What is all the excitement?" asks Akua feeling quite irritated.

Akua suddenly spots a parrot sitting next to Soso doing exactly what Soso is doing and it sounds like someone is saying exactly what Akua is saying to Soso!

That really makes Akua wonder. "Ah, I see what you've been trying to tell me Soso!" Akua shouts, "It's a parrot who's been copying me all this time. Now I have another friend and we'll call him Copycat Parrot!"

AKUA, SOSO AND COPYCAT PARROT GO TO THE MARKET

Written by Akua Adoma

It is a bright sunny day when Akua rises from bed fresh, joyful, and full of mischief.

Akua runs onto the veranda and says to Soso and Copycat parrot "Let's have a day out at the market, it will be fun!"

Soso turns to Copycat parrot saying, "Mmmmm we will meet other people and can buy lots of fruits and nuts"

Copycat parrot looks like he has a plan up his sleeve and stretches his wings after a good night sleep. Soso turns his head towards Copycat parrot and Akua calls out to her mum "Mama could you please give me and my friends a lift into town to the market? Mama is more than happy to do so and gives Akua a shopping list, for tomatoes, peppers, bananas, oranges, rice, nuts, spinach, plantain, and potatoes.

AKUA, SOSO AND COPYCAT PARROT GO TO THE MARKET

Mama, Akua, Soso and Copycat Parrot get into the family orange car. Mama drops them off at the market and calls out to Akua to be ready to be picked up in an hour at the same spot where she dropped them off. There are cars and buses stuck in the traffic and people whizzing up and down the street in between the cars going about their business. This is so much fun and Akua, Soso and Copycat get rather excited. It is not often they get out into the town on a busy market day.

Filled with mischief and excitement Akua, Soso perched on her shoulder and Copycat Parrot on her other shoulder head off with the shopping list and start at the tomato stall and then to the plantain stall. Soso and Copycat Parrot shout at the same time "Gosh the plantain looks like a huge banana!" Akua bargains with the lady at the stall and manages to get three bananas for one cedi.

Next is the stall where they sell vegetables. Akua asks the tomato stall owner "how much are these tomatoes in the front row?" and the stall owner replies, "a cedi for the lot please". Soso tickles Akua's ears as if to say he cannot wait to eat them!

Soso suddenly jumps off Akua's shoulder and onto the table of tomatoes causing a bit of a nuisance and the Stall owner shouting "get off, get off my tomatoes!" Soso jumps off and gets a telling off from Akua who is ruffled by all this. Her hair is now in a mess where Copycat Parrot has tried getting back onto her shoulder and falls flat on her head messing Akua's hair up and almost getting tangled in it. "Awwwchh!" exclaimed Akua. "Get out of my hair, get out of my hair!"

Other people in the market were not sure what was happening as Soso started to do a dance and Copycat parrot of course copying every move Soso made. The whole market was now at a standstill to watch, using their pots and pans to tap a lovely tune to what they thought was a show put on for them! Akua joined in. She just could not help herself! They were enjoying themselves so much they forgot all about getting Mama's shopping!

It was time to get back to be picked up. No shopping had been done! Akua panicked and had to think very quickly. She gathered Soso and Copycat parrot up and whispered to them "you need to help me sort the mess out and get the shopping Mama asked for.

With a skip and a stride Soso picked up the shopping basket and asked Akua to follow him, he went from one stall to another bargaining with the stall holders. Copycat parrot was busy sorting out and tidying up the mess. In no time the shopping was done, and the mess cleared up, Akua, Soso and Copycat Parrot were back just where Mama had dropped them off earlier and ready to be picked up.

Mama came round the corner, stopped to let Akua, Soso and Copycat Parrot into the car with all the shopping. Not a word was said about the fun they had had in the market although they were bursting to tell Mama everything.

Driving back home with the wind blowing in their faces, smiling away and mischief in their eyes, Mama could not help thinking she must have missed something at the market! Akua was secretly thinking of their next adventure.

CPSIA information can be obtained
at www.ICGtesting.com
Printed in the USA
BVHW020942290421
606136BV00009B/863